About This Book

Title: *Lucky Rat*

Step: 3

Word Count: 292

Skills in Focus: sh and th

Tricky Words: Coach Shea, could, forward, gymnast, lucky, should, through, would

Ideas For Using This Book

Before Reading:
- **Comprehension:** Look at the title and cover image together. Ask the readers to make a prediction. Ask students to share if they have something they believe brings them luck.
- **Accuracy:** Practice the tricky words listed on Page 1.
- **Phonemic Awareness:** Tell students they will be reading words with the digraphs *sh* and *th*. Explain that a digraph is two letters that make one sound. Practice taking apart and putting together the sounds in *fish*. How many sounds are in the word *fish*? What is the first sound? Middle sound? End sound? Say the word *fish* again and ask the students to put their hands in the air when they hear the /*sh*/ sound. Repeat with the word *show*. Continue with *th*, using the words *thick* and *cloth*.
- **Vocabulary:** Tell students that *thud* means a heavy fall and a *mascot* is a symbol for a group that is thought to bring luck.

During Reading:
- Have the students point under each word as they read it.
- **Decoding:** If stuck on a word, help students say each sound and blend it together smoothly.
- **Comprehension:** Invite students to add to or change their predictions from before reading.

After Reading:
Discuss the book. Some ideas for questions:
- What happens to Pam when Jax is not nearby?
- Why does Pam want Jax to go with her to the gym show?
- Did Jax really bring Pam good luck in the show? Why or why not?

Lucky Rat

Text by Leanna Koch

Educational Content by
Kristen Cowen

Illustrated by
Mike Byrne

PICTURE WINDOW BOOKS
a capstone imprint

Pam, Ben, Max, and Sam are best pals. Pam has Jax the rat. Ben has Rex the dog.

Sam has Dot the cat. Max has Fran the fish. The friends play with their pets together.

Pam is a gymnast.

Pam can flip, spin, and jump.

But, if Jax is not nearby,
Pam lands flips with a
crash and a thud.

Pam is lost if her lucky rat,
Jax, is not close.

Pam is in a rush to get to
the big gym show. "I wish
I could take you with me,"
Pam tells Jax.

Jax will stick with Pam
through thick and thin.

"I should hide Jax," Pam thinks.
"I can stash him in this sock."

Pam tucks Jax in her sock.

Pam puts Jax in a cloth bag
and shuts it. Jax is squished.
Jax yelps. Pam opens the bag
and tells Jax to hush.

It's time to hit the mats for the big show. Pam thinks of Jax.

Pam puts the bag next to the mat.

Pam's pals wish her well.

Pam steps up to the mat.

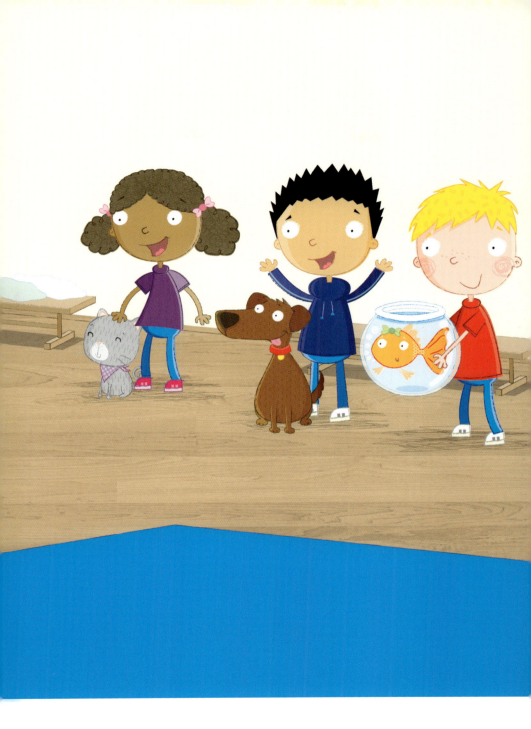

"You can do this!" Pam's pals yell.

"This is it!" Pam thinks.

In a flash, Pam rushes
forward, jumps, and flips.

Pam's pals gush with pride.

Pam is thrilled. She did well.
"I must tell Jax," Pam thinks.

"Jax!" Pam calls to the cloth
bag. Jax is not in the bag!

Jax is not in his sock.
"Jax is lost!" Pam yells.

"Is this Jax?" Coach Shea asks.

"That's Jax!" Pam says. "Thanks."

"Next time, your pals can keep Jax with them," Coach tells Pam.

28

"I think that is a good plan,"
Pam nods.

"Jax would be a good mat
rat mascot for the club," Pam
jokes. "He is a lucky mat rat!"

More Ideas:

Practicing Digraph th and sh:

Use bingo chips (or any other small objects such as beads) to practice segmenting words with digraphs *th* and *sh*. For each word, say it to the students and have them slowly stretch out the sounds, sliding one chip as they say each sound. Tell students to run their fingers across the chips to blend the word back together.

Optional: Challenge students to determine the number of sounds in the word and how many chips they will need.

Suggested Words:
sh: *fish, crash, rush, stash, shut, hush, show, wish, flash, gush*
th: *thud, thick, thin, cloth, Smith, think, thrill*

Extended Learning Activity

Change the Story:
Think about the story. Imagine that you could change an event and make it your favorite part of the story. What would happen differently? Draw a picture to show the new story event. Share it with a friend and tell them why it would be your favorite part of the story.

Published by Picture Window Books,
an imprint of Capstone
1710 Roe Crest Drive,
North Mankato, Minnesota 56003
capstonepub.com

Lucky Rat was originally published as
The Lucky Charm, copyright 2011 by Picture Window Books.

Library of Congress Cataloging-in-Publication Data is available
on the Library of Congress website.

ISBN: 9780756596439 (hardback)
ISBN: 9780756585907 (paperback)
ISBN: 9780756590505 (eBook PDF)

Printed and bound in the USA. 5757